T. H. Morrell

A Sketch of the Life of James William Wallack

T. H. Morrell

A Sketch of the Life of James William Wallack

ISBN/EAN: 9783337017248

Printed in Europe, USA, Canada, Australia, Japan

Cover: Foto ©Raphael Reischuk / pixelio.de

More available books at **www.hansebooks.com**

WALLACK.

A
SKETCH OF THE LIFE

OF

JAMES WILLIAM WALLACK,

(SENIOR,)

LATE ACTOR AND MANAGER.

"   *   *   *   ; and the elements
So mix'd in him, that nature might stand up
And say to all the world, — *This was a Man !*"

SHAKESPEARE.

NEW YORK:

T. H. MORRELL,

184 Fulton Street.

1865.

. Edition, 250 Copies, of which 50 are on Large Paper.

BERGEN & TRIPP, PRINTERS.

PREFACE.

THE following pages have been compiled and printed in this shape, at the solicitation of a number of the friends and admirers of the late lamented artist whose name appears upon the title page, they being desirous of preserving a suitable memorial in some neat and durable form.

The compiler makes no pretensions to originality in the preparation of this sketch; a great portion of the matter having been gathered and transcribed, with some variations, and numerous additions, from the various obituary notices that appeared in the newspapers of the day, and more particularly in the columns of the *New York Tribune* and *Herald*.

He has, also, had recourse to several journals, cotemporary with Mr. WALLACK, when in the "zenith of his popularity," and also to a number of volumes of dramatic reminiscences published in this country during the past few years.

Should, therefore, this hurriedly-prepared Memoir, in its imperfect state, meet with the commendation of even a *few* of such as are interested in a history of the professional career of the late Mr. WALLACK, the desire of the compiler will have been more than gratified.

New York, January, 1865.

MEMORIAL.

 AMES WILLIAM WALLACK was born in London, at Hercules Buildings, Lambeth, on the 24th of August, 1795. His parents had both attained distinction upon the stage; his father, WILLIAM WALLACK, being a celebrated comedian and vocalist, while his mother, whose maiden name was ELIZABETH FIELD, had played the leading female characters with GARRICK for several years.

It was their intention that their son JAMES should enter the navy, and at an early age he received his appointment as midshipman; but his fondness for his father's profession, to which he was irresistibly attracted, induced him speedily to renounce all ideas of following the perilous fortunes of a sea-faring life, and he therefore became soon after a member of the Academic Theatre, established by Queen CHARLOTTE, in Leicester Street, where English and German children appeared on alternate nights.

It is said that when only four years of age he made his first appearance on any stage, at the Royal Circus, in a fairy spectacle. It was during one of the performances of the 'Academicals' that his earnest and vigorous impersonations attracted the attention of the distinguished Irish orator and dramatist, RICHARD BRINSLEY SHERIDAN, who, in consequence, was influential in obtaining for him, then only twelve years of age, an engagement at Drury Lane Theatre. He here remained attached to the regular company, steadily rising in public favor, until the destruction of that building by fire, which occurred on the night of the 24th February, 1809.

He soon after went to Ireland, but shortly returned, and at the age of eighteen, appeared on the occasion of the opening of the New Theatre Royal, Drury Lane, as *Laertes* to the *Hamlet* of the eccentric ROBERT WILLIAM ELLISTON.

He subsequently, during the engagement of EDMUND KEAN, supported him with great ability, having been assigned such characters as Iago, Edgar, Macduff, Richmond, and others, second only in importance to those of the great tragedian of the day.

About this time, 1817, his marriage with the daughter of the celebrated actor, Mr. JOHN JOHN-STONE, familiarly known as "Irish Johnstone," took place, and he shortly thereafter, through the intervention of his personal friend, Lord BYRON, who was a member of the Drury board of direc-tors, having obtained two years leave of absence from that Theatre, departed on his first visit to the shores of America.

He made his *debut* in the city of New York, at the Park Theatre, in the character of *Macbeth*, on the 7th of September, 1818. His success was instantaneous and decided, his reception by a house crowded to its utmost capacity, being of the most enthusiastic description.

On the 30th of November, he appeared, for the first time, in Boston, as *Rolla*, (in Sheridan's popular play of *Pizarro*,) his impersonation of which character being pronounced one of the finest specimens of melo-dramatic acting ever witnessed in America; and, with the exception of JOHN PHILIP KEMBLE's, probably unrivalled on the other side of the Atlantic. Commended by the warm admiration of his own countrymen, and with the advantage, too, of the endorsement of the New York public, with whom his popularity was convincingly established, he was flatteringly received in the "Athens of America," and was, on all occasions, greeted by full and appreciative houses.

During this season he also performed engagements in Baltimore and Philadelphia, appearing as Rolla, Macbeth, Octavian, Richard, etc., and playing in the latter city for thirteen nights, receiving at his first benefit the handsome sum of fifteen hundred and twenty dollars.

Renewing his engagement in that city, (Philadelphia,) for seven additional nights, he gave, with great approbation, Bertram, Richard II., Don Felix, etc., etc., and on his benefit, the following imitations: *Kemble* as *Rolla, Munden* as

Peter in "The Cabinet," *Betty* as *Young Norval,* *Matthews* as *Buskin, Rae* as *Ordonio, Cooke* as *Richard, Fawcett* as *Blanchard* in "John Bull," *Kean* as *Shylock,* and *Incledon* as *Hawthorn.*

His elder brother, Mr. HENRY WALLACK, also performed in Baltimore, in this year, it being his first appearance in the United States.

This gentleman still survives, at the age of seventy-two, and is now, I believe, residing in London.

In 1819 Mr. WALLACK played a prosperous engagement in Savannah, Ga., and in the same year his eldest son, Mr. JOHN LESTER WALLACK, (the stage manager and leading actor, and now the sole proprietor, of his father's theatre in Broadway,) was born.

For two years Mr. WALLACK appeared in almost the entire range of his characters, among which were *Hamlet, Richard, Coriolanus, Don Felix,* (in the *Wonder,*) *Martin Heywood,* (in the *Rent Day,*) and *Massaroni,* (in the *Brigand,*) a role so admirably portrayed by his talented son above-mentioned, a few years since, at the old theatre on the corner of Broadway and Broome street, and which produced at the time so great an impression, electrifying his audiences, and reviving in the minds of old play-goers the halcyon days of his father.

. Mr. JAMES H. HACKETT, so well known from his original and able representation of Falstaff, in his recent work published in this city, and entitled "Notes and Comments on Shakespeare," referring to our actor's first appearance in this country, says:

. "Mr. WALLACK then seemed not more than twenty-five years of age, came directly from Drury Lane, where he had already attained a high rank in a profession then graced by many eminent artists; and the season of 1818 was Mr. WALLACK's first in America.   His figure and personal bearing on or off the stage were very *distingué;* his eye was sparkling; his hair dark, curly, and luxuriant; his facial features finely chiselled; and together with the natural conformation of his head, throat, and chest, Mr. WALLACK presented a remarkable specimen of manly beauty.   He at once became, and continued to be, — during visits which were repeated, occasionally protracted, and were seldom separated by intervals longer than a theatrical season or two each, and for a term of more than twenty years, — one of the greatest and most invariably attractive favorites furnished the American by the British stage.

"With particular reference to Mr. WALLACK'S *Hamlet*, which, as it has happened, I have not had an opportunity to witness since my youth, when my ideas of the character were crude and superficial, and which, therefore, it would be unjust in me now to criticise retrospectively, I did then very well note that Mr. WALLACK'S action was easy and graceful; his voice and articulation were clear and distinct; and though from the impression it made, and which I still retain of that early-seen performance, it might, according to my later and more matured ideal, have lacked a sufficiency of *weight* in the philosophical portions, and also of depth and intensity of meditation in the soliloquies, it was then unanimously approved and a special favorite with the New York public. Mr. WALLACK, besides being popular in a number of leading tragic parts, was esteemed without an equal as *Don Felix* in the comedy of *The Wonder*,

and throughout the range of genteel and high-
spirited comedy generally, as also in a number of
melo-dramatic characters.

"His *Martin Heywood* in "*The Rent Day*,"
Massaroni in "*The Brigand*," and his *Don Cæsar
de Bazan* in later years, manifested a high and
exquisite order of art; while those who in Mr.
WALLACK's early days saw his *Rolla* in the play
of "*Pizarro*" can never forget that it was unap-
proached by any other performer, and the most
remarkably picturesque, fascinating and continu-
ally attractive performance then known to the
American stage.

"In versatility of talent, probably the stage has
never had any other actor capable of satisfying the
public in such a *variety* of prominent characters;
his costumes, too, were remarkably characteristic,
and always in admirable taste, and Mr. WALLACK,
in every respect, has proved himself a complete
master of the histrionic art."

> " His was the gifted eye, which grace still touch'd
> As if with second nature; and his dreams,
> His childish dreams, were lit by hues of heaven—
> Those which make Genius."
>
> *Miss Landon.*

After realizing considerable in amount, and his popularity much increased, he, after two years of unprecedented success, returned to England, again appearing at Drury Lane, where he was cordially welcomed by the friends and companions of his earlier days. Remaining, however, but a single season, he again visited America, in the year 1822, to be as before the recipient of a most brilliant and flattering reception.

It was during this visit that while journeying to Philadelphia, having been announced to appear at the Walnut Street Theatre, as *Hamlet*, the stage-coach in which he travelled was overturned, and he suffered a compound fracture of the leg, which incapacitated him for his professional duties for the space of eighteen months, and the effect of which was always partially discernible throughout his life. When he had sufficiently recovered from this unfortunate check to his labors and his triumphs, he again departed for England, leaving however, his wardrobe, etc., *in* New York, in which city he resolved *only*, if *ever* again, to make his re-appearance.

And kind Fortune, his patron Saint during a

long and honorable life, destined that he should again appear on the boards of the old Park, after an absence of nearly two years.

The New York public had evinced profound regret at his misfortune, and now assembled in overwhelming numbers to express their sympathy and to extend to him an earnest welcome, all the more hearty and sincere because of a general conviction that his thorough recovery was impossible, and that his future career must be limited to the representation of a few exceptional parts.

He was announced to appear in two plays, and as he hobbled upon the stage on crutches, in the character of Captain Bertram, (an old sailor,) the apprehensions of his friends seemed realized, and there were audible manifestations of pity from the audience, who were moved with grief to see the favorite artist thus apparently deprived of the free use of his limbs.

The expression of surprise and enthusiasm may be readily imagined when, in the second piece — "My Aunt"— he bounded upon the stage, as *Dick Dashall*, with the elasticity and vigor that had been wont to distinguish him in his earlier engagements.

About this period Mr. WALLACK, during his stay in England, became stage manager of Drury Lane (BOOTH having retired) under ELLISTON, occasionally playing leading parts; and, it is said, he was several times honored by invitations to act at the royal palace.

He also belonged at this time to the Garrick Club, at which a fine bust of him is still preserved, and he was associated with some of the most distinguished men of the time. In 1827 he played *Othello* to the *Iago* of EDMUND KEAN.

A memorable event in the history of the English stage occurred in the year 1828, (in which Mr. WALLACK was one of the prominent movers,) and which is but another proof of the kindly feeling evinced by the members of the dramatic profession towards their brother actors when in the hour of need and distress.

It was the occasion of the farewell benefit and last appearance in public of poor old JOE GRIMALDI, the *Garrick of clowns*, who was compelled, on account of severe and protracted bodily infirmities, to bid adieu to the profession to which he had been attached for so many years.   Among those who took an especial interest in making arrangements for this much needed testimonial, no one was more indefatigable in his exertions, and rendered more efficient aid, than our young actor, who exerted himself as much as he could have done if the night had been his own.

· The affair came off at Drury Lane on the night of the 28th of June, 1828, the performances consisting of a number of popular pieces, concluding with the *Harlequin Hoax*, in which Mr. GRIMALDI, after repeating his famous rendition of the jester, sang his last song, and with the delivery of a farewell address made his final bow to the public.

The benefit exceeded the most sanguine expectations, realizing a clear profit of two hundred and seventy pounds sterling.

The old man survived but a few years, and died in 1837, having left as a legacy to his profession the memoirs of his life, which he had written in his latter days, and which have since been published, running through a number of editions.

Shortly after, in 1828, Mr. WALLACK again meditated making a trip to this country.

On the occasion of the closing of the Drury Lane Theatre for the season he was presented by his fellow actors of that establishment, over which he had presided as their manager for three years, with a handsome service of plate, accompanied by a feeling address, which was delivered by the cele-brated comedian, Mr. CHARLES MATTHEWS.

It was indeed a deserving tribute of respect and esteem, and the highest compliment to the impar-tial and honorable manner in which he had dis-charged his arduous and numerous duties.

He was accompanied on his voyage to New York, in September of this year, by the favorite and *distinguished* actress, Mrs. BARNES, and soon after his arrival appeared, as usual, at the "Drury of America," drawing fuller houses than any pre-ceding performer of that season.

In November he played an engagement in Philadelphia, at the Arch Street Theatre, under the
management of Mr. Wood, that gentleman offering
him two hundred dollars per night for his services,
Mr. Forrest being the counter attraction at the
Walnut, receiving the same compensation.

Cooper, the tragedian, was then also performing
at the Chestnut Street Theatre.

Thus were three theatres struggling in that city
for existence; a bitter spirit of rivalry existing
between the managers, who were striving with
ceaseless and unflinching energy each to outvie
in attraction and popularity the establishment of
the other, and making the most fearful sacrifices
to overthrow professionally his opponent.

In December, the 'war of the managers,' having ceased, Mr. Wallack played for a few nights
at the Chestnut, and then returned to New York.

On the 7th of January, 1829, was performed
for the first time in America, at the Park Theatre,
Miss Mary Russell Mitford's new tragedy of *Rienzi*, introducing Mr. Wallack in the role of the

hero — and quoting from a periodical of the day, devoted to "literature, the drama and the fine arts," we find the following:

* * * * * * * * Mr. WALLACK'S Rienzi was good throughout — often excellent — and some passages given in a style that we conceive could not well be improved by any man. His conception of the character appeared to us correct — his action free and graceful — his articulation clear and distinct; and at times there was a fire and energy thrown into some of the spirit-stirring harangues that went home to the heart, whilst the domestic scenes with his daughter were replete with delicate touches of nature and feeling. * * * * * * * In characters of an heroic or romantic cast, when the moral feelings of the audience are enlisted on his side, there is no man like him, —

> " A love of right, a scorn of wrong,
> Are written on his manly brow and in his manly eye,"—

while a voice, "rich in its mellow depth," pours forth the glowing sentiments of his author with a fervor and feeling that well nigh approach perfection. "

Rienzi was revived by Mr. WALLACK at the same theatre, in 1836, in all its original splendor, and subsequently at his charming little house in Broadway, corner of Broome Street, where it attracted for a succession of nights immense audiences, including many old play-goers, who had witnessed its first representation. In 1832 (in the interim visiting his native land,) he played a number of engagements in this city; and the following brief extracts, from an article written for the Sunday Times, entitled " *The* " *Old* " *Park Theatre, by an Ex-Reporter,*" and appearing in the columns of that journal a few years ago, may not be uninteresting at this time.

"On Monday, September 3d, Mr. JAMES WAL-LACK—*the* WALLACK—commenced an engagement with 'Pizarro' and 'My Aunt,' and drew eight hundred and twenty dollars and fifty cents. * * * * * On Wednesday, Mr. WALLACK's second night, 'The Rent Day' and 'Spring and Autumn' were performed to six hundred and fifty dollars and seventy-five cents. On Thursday, he, with the Ravels, drew a fair house—five hundred and fifty dollars and seventy-five cents. On Friday, Mr. WALLACK played in the 'Rent Day' and 'Spring and Autumn,' to six hundred and eighteen dollars and twenty-five cents, and on Saturday he appeared to four hundred and forty-seven dollars.

On Monday, September 10th, Mr. WALLACK repeated 'Pizarro' and 'My Aunt,' to four hundred and ninety-six dollars. On Tuesday, 'The Rent Day' and 'The Adopted Child' were played to five hundred and twenty dollars. On Wednesday, Mr. HACKETT played to seven hundred and fifteen dollars and twenty-five cents, and on Thursday Mr. WALLACK appeared to four hundred and ten dollars and seventy-five cents.

On Friday, 'The Brigand,' 'The Rent Day,' and 'The Adopted Child,' drew one thousand forty-eight dollars and fifty cents, being Mr. WALLACK's benefit. On Saturday, Mr. HACKETT played 'Rip Van Winkle,' Brother Jonathan, etc., to three hundred and fifty-seven dollars and twenty-five cents."

He was succeeded by Mr. CHARLES KEMBLE, and subsequently by Miss FANNY KEMBLE, and in October was re-engaged, performing his usual line of characters, and appearing in connection with Miss CLARA FISHER (now Mrs. MAEDER,) for whose benefit he performed *Don Felix* in 'The Wonder' on the evening of the 1st of November; Master BURKE playing also on the same night. Receipts eight hundred and twenty-five dollars and seventy-five cents.

In 1835 Mr. WALLACK made a professional trip to Baltimore. His engagement at the Holiday Street Theatre lasted however but a few nights, the good people of the 'Monumental city,' for some unaccountable cause, not extending to him on this occasion the cordial and enthusiastic patronage that had uniformly been accorded him.

This apparent coolness, so unexpected and uncalled for, without having any tendency to dishearten our actor, did not fail to produce a strong impression on him; his not too sensitive, yet impulsive nature, prompted him to speak, on the evening of his last appearance, his own views on the subject, unreservedly and with frankness.

His address to the audience is here given *verbatim*.

"LADIES AND GENTLEMEN: — I appear before
you at your call. I am unaccustomed to extem-
poraneous speaking; but however reluctant I
may usually be to address a public audience, I
am free to confess, that I never felt more embarrassment than on the present occasion. I am but
a plain man, and speak the words of truth, not-
withstanding my profession leads me to assume
the garb of fiction. If I were to tell you that I
leave Baltimore gratified, I should tell you a lie
— for, of the ten nights I have played in this city,
this is the only audience I have had the pleasure
of witnessing, and you have my sincere thanks for
honoring my name by your appearance this evening. I am aware of the duties — of far more
importance to you than my poor services — that
have prevented your honoring me with your attendance, which otherwise, if I may be allowed to
judge by the audiences I have received in other
cities, would, I doubt not, have been more general. I therefore repeat, that I thank you most
kindly for doing me the honor you have, by appearing here to night; and, with the hope that
when I may come among you again I shall at
least occasionally see such an audience as the one
before me, I bid you farewell."

He then returned to New York, and appeared at the Park Theatre.

From the "*Ex-Reporter's Journal*" we again extract :

"On Wednesday (Oct. 21st, 1835,) Mr. WALLACK commenced another engagement, and played in 'Pizarro' and 'My Aunt,' to nine hundred and nineteen dollars and fifty cents.   *   *   Miss PHILLIPS appeared with Mr. WALLACK on Saturday, in 'The Hunchback,' ('The Brigand' being the after-piece,) to eight hundred and eighty-four dollars and seventy-five cents.

Monday, Oct. 26th, 'The Wife' and 'Spring and Autumn,' with Mr. WALLACK and Miss PHILLIPS, drew five hundred and seventy-two dollars.

On Tuesday, Mr. PLACIDE took a benefit, and paid Mr. SIMPSON five hundred dollars for the house, etc.   The receipts were about six hundred and twenty dollars.

The 'Merchant of Venice' and the 'Brigand'

on Wednesday drew six hundred and nineteen dollars. * * * *

Mr. WALLACK took a benefit and closed his engagement on Friday. 'The Rent Day,' 'Spring and Autumn,' and 'The Adopted Child' were played, and although a heavy storm prevailed, the rain falling in torrents, the receipts amounted to one thousand and forty dollars and twenty-five cents."

Re-appeared in November for a few nights, *Yankee Hill* performing alternately with him.

On the evening of the 21st of December, 1835, while the public mind had scarcely recovered from the shock occasioned by the recent dreadful calamity which had visited the city in the form of the most extensive and terrible conflagration that had ever occurred in this country, Mr. WALLACK again commenced an engagement, and though appearing in two of his most popular characters, *Rolla* and *Dick Dashall*, the receipts were only three hundred and seven dollars and seventy-five cents, undoubtedly owing to the still depressed state of the public heart, and the excessively cold weather combined, the thermometer being, during that memorable month, frequently down to zero.

It will not probably be amiss to here state that the receipts at the Park Theatre on the night of the fire, December 16th, were only one hundred and fifty-four dollars, the weather being the coldest of the season.

On Christmas night, just *twenty-nine* years ago from the date of the death of the lamented subject of this memoir, he appeared in his favorite role of the 'Brigand,' which, — together with the spectacle of the 'Virgin of the Sun,' and a ballet, — constituted the evening's performances, and drew one thousand one hundred and forty-three dollars and twenty-five cents.

But too many statistics may weary the readers of this little sketch, and we will therefore briefly refer to Mr. WALLACK's subsequent career.

On the 11th of January, 1836, he appeared in Philadelphia for the benefit of his friend, Mr. WILLIAM B. WOOD, another distinguished veteran actor and manager, "now gone to his long home."

In the same year, played in New York several engagements, (always at the Park,) appearing as *Shylock*, *St. Pierre*, etc., and reviving *Rienzi* as referred to above.

Mr. HAMBLIN also produced the same piece at the Bowery Theatre, in gorgeous style, and we believe it was also brought out about the same time at the old Franklin Theatre.

In the month of May of this year, Mr. WALLACK took passage for Europe, previous to which however he adopted the example set him by others of his profession, and more particularly the then rising "Star of the American Stage," Mr. EDWIN FORREST, (through whose munificence and patronage our dramatic literature has been so enriched, and to whom the American stage is indebted for the popular plays of 'The Gladiator' and 'The Broker of Bogota,' by Dr. R. M. BIRD, 'Metamora,' by Mr. JOHN AUGUSTUS STONE, etc., etc.,) and offered a premium for an original play to be constructed especially in view of his peculiar style of acting.

The following letter addressed to the editor of

the New York Mirror, the late General GEORGE
P. MORRIS, will be read with interest in this connection.

PACKET SHIP SHEFFIELD, }
May 28*th*, 1836. }

MY DEAR SIR :

I am most anxious to procure, on my return to
the United States, an original play by a native
author, and on some striking and powerful American subject.   Of course, I am desirous that the
principal character should be made prominent,
and adapted to me and my dramatick capabilities,
such as they may happen to be.   Will you be
kind enough to offer for such a production the
sum of *one thousand dollars*, which I will pay to
any writer who will present the best piece of the
description alluded to.   All manuscripts will be
submitted to a committee of literary gentlemen of
your city, and to the author of the play selected
by them will be adjudged the premium just speci-
fied.   Be kind enough to insert the enclosed advertisement in the Mirror; and, with very many
thanks for the kind manner in which you have in-

terested yourself in this matter for me, I am, my
dear sir, your obliged and faithful servant,

JAMES WALLACK.

To GEORGE P. MORRIS, Esq.,
.Editor of the Mirror.

The following is the advertisement referred to:

TO NATIVE DRAMATICK AUTHORS.

The subscriber offers the sum of *one thousand
dollars* for the best original play upon an attractive and striking subject in American history.
The principal part to be adapted to his style of
acting. A committee of literary gentlemen will
be chosen to decide upon the merits of such plays
as may be submitted to them for this premium;
which will be awarded to the writer of the best
production of the above description. It is re-
quested that all manuscripts may be sent, (post
paid,) on or before the first of October next, addressed to GEORGE P. MORRIS, Esq., New York
Mirror Office.

JAMES WALLACK.

Whether in desiring thus to encourage the dramatic talent of this country, his generous offer met with its merited appreciation, and the anticipated result at this time, the compiler is not aware, although several years after Mr. WALLACK appeared in an original play, written expressly for him by Mr. N. P. WILLIS, and which will be noticed hereafter in these pages.

On his return to New York a few months after, he played an engagement at the National Theatre, corner of Church and Leonard Streets, and in the following year undertook the management of this house, selecting the finest company probably ever gathered together in any place of amusement in this city, not excepting, I think, even that subsequently congregated at "Old Wallack's." This theatre, (the National,) was re-opened under Mr. WALLACK'S auspices, on the 28th of August, 1837, his brother, HENRY, acting as stage-manager.

To those familiar with the sterling ability, judicious taste and liberality displayed by Mr. WALLACK in his managerial capacity during the past twelve years, it is hardly necessary to state that the 'drooping fortunes of the old National

were again revived,' and that it was soon established as one of the favorite resorts of our amuse-
ment-loving citizens.   And to the enterprising
spirit of Mr. WALLACK alone could be attributed
the signal success achieved at this theatre.

At the National, during our manager's control-
ling influence, appeared among others, the charming opera troupe, so favorably remembered, and
consisting of the SEGUINS, Miss SHIRREFF, DE
BEGNIS, WILSON, etc., etc., Madame CELESTE,
VANDENHOFF, HACKETT, etc.

And besides Mr. WALLACK himself occasionally
acting, his brother HENRY, together with his son
J. W. WALLACK, Jr., (now one of the finest
melo-dramatic actors on the stage,) also frequently performed.

In April, 1839, Mr. WALLACK produced at the
National N. P. WILLIS's new play of 'Tortesa
the Usurer,' himself sustaining the principal
character, which, as before stated, had been written especially for him.

This play was presented in superb style, the

scenic arrangements evincing in all their appoint-
ments, the same liberal spirit of profuse expendi-
ture which had characterised every production of
the season, and it met with marked success, keep-
ing possession of the stage for several weeks.

Prior to his leaving for England, in this month,
he was tendered by his friends and admirers a
complimentary benefit, at which the inimitable
comedian, Mr. W. E. BURTON, volunteered to perform, coming from Philadelphia expressly for that
purpose, and appearing as Sir *Simon Slack* in
'Spring and Autumn,' Mr. WALLACK playing also in the same piece.

The beneficiary, then, as on every similar occasion, had no cause to complain of the brilliant
ovation accorded him.

Mr. WALLACK immediately sailed for England,
in the steamship Great Western, returning in a
few weeks after in the same vessel. He soon however made another trip, introducing at the Surrey
theatre 'Tortesa,' supported by the accomplished actress, Mrs. VINING; and although he was suffering from illness, it is said "he played with far

more fire than usual, and drew down thunders of applause." The play was also highly successful, and was repeated for many nights to large audiences. During the ensuing season, Mr. EDWIN FORREST played a brilliant engagement at the National, under Mr. WALLACK's management, the house having been completely renovated and repaired, and presenting, on its re-opening, a beautiful appearance, "resplendent with glittering decorations of gold, and tasteful paintings."

Mr. CHARLES KEAN (son of the eminent tragedian,) played an engagement at this house at the close of Mr. FORREST's, but was unfortunately compelled to temporarily relinquish it, owing to a sudden fit of illness.

In September of this year, resulting thus far so prosperously for the management, this beautiful theatre,—which Mr. WALLACK had endeavored so arduously to render one of the most attractive places of amusement in the city, introducing as he did the most refined and elevated entertainments, and rivalling in popularity the old Park Theatre,— was totally destroyed by fire. And in no better terms can an idea of that unfortunate event be conveyed to the mind of the reader, than by the insertion here of the following graphic account by an eye-witness, published in one of the weekly journals of that period :

"Seldom is it that we are inclined to visit the scene of a conflagration, but so strong an interest did we feel for those who would suffer from the destruction of the once beautiful National, that so soon as we learned it was that edifice on fire we fell into the current of thousands who were hastening to the spot.

"We found the entire house completely enveloped — the flames flashing upward, fifty feet above the walls, and roaring like a cataract. The safety of the adjoining buildings, now occupied the attention of the intrepid firemen, who were making every exertion in their power to rescue them from the raging, devouring element. As yet the beautiful French church was untouched, and its marble walls and zinc dome, it was hoped would save it, though so much exposed.

"With a friend, who from boyhood has clambered the giddy mast, we passed up through the

house adjoining the church to a flight of steps
leading across an alley to the roof of that classic
model of a Christian Temple.   From this elevation we could see down into the very interior of
the Theatre, which presented the appearance of a
huge cauldron of molten gold, bubbling and sway-
ing from side to side with terrific fury.

"The summit of the dome of the church was sur-
mounted by a "lantern," that has been the admiration of all lovers of architecture.   Fatal to this
classic edifice was this crowning beauty.   While
we were standing on its roof, this wooden lantern,
heated almost to ignition, took fire from a spark.
At this moment to an unmoved spectator the
church presented the most beautiful sight imagin-
able.   Totally uninjured stood this specimen of
the simple Ionic architecture, graceful in all its
proportions, with an air of purity divine, from the
whiteness of the marble, well suited to the worship
to which it was devoted, when there burst forth a
vivid light from the summit of its lantern, that for
nearly one hour was the only portion of the building on fire.   A true " fire-worshipper" would
have unconsciously fallen on his knees in adoration,
could he have seen this manifestation of the god

he worships.   We never saw anything more beautiful and impressive.

"At length this treacherous ornament conveyed
the fire to the dome, and we now found it getting
uncomfortable to remain longer at this dizzy height,
and the excitement for a moment was somewhat intense, when we recollected that the flight of stairs
by which we came must be cut away to prevent
the fire being communicated to the adjoining house,
occupied by the worthy Pastor of the church.

"We hurriedly passed this bridge, —*not* "of
sighs,"—though it reminded us of that Venitian
structure, and met the energetic fireman, with axe
in hand, to demolish this connecting link, which
purpose he soon effected.

"Three churches, as many private buildings, together with the Theatre, were now on fire, and
the scene, from an adjoining house-top was grand
in the extreme.

"It is from no lack of sympathy with the unfortunate sufferers, that we have thus alluded to this
sad catastrophe.   Most sincerely do we participate

with the entire community in sorrowing for their loss, and most ready shall we be found to lend every aid in our power to further any plan adopted for the relief of those so suddenly deprived of the means of exercising their profession."

A few evenings after this lamentable occurrence, some three hundred of the most enterprising citizens of this city, met at the Astor House to testify their sympathy and continued friendship for Mr. WALLACK, and with the intention of devising some plan where by a new Theatre could be erected, and placed under his management.

Thus encouraged, Mr. WALLACK immediately transferred his company to the theatre connected with Niblo's Garden, and it is needless to say that his commendable course, which displayed, under the trying circumstances, an uncommon degree of fortitude and perseverance, was promptly responded to by the public, and he was, with his company, greeted by an immense concourse of sympathizing friends, eager to demonstrate their appreciation of his talents as manager and actor, and his worth as a man.

His prosperity, however, was of short duration.
Mr. and Miss VANDERHOOF, having been previous-
ly engaged to play at the old theatre, soon after appeared here, achieving considerable success, by
their original and finished representations, and were
followed by Mr. CHARLES KEAN, etc. but after an
energetic struggle of a few weeks only, against a
then unfortunate location, the disadvantages of a
cramped house, and the severities of the times, Mr.
WALLACK threw open his theatre for the last time,
on Monday evening, November 18th, 1839, Mr.
FORREST appearing on the occasion, as *Macbeth.*

At the close of the tragedy, Mr. WALLACK an-
swered the call of the audience, by coming forward,
evidently much affected by the enthusiastic cheer-
ing, yet sufficiently self-possessed to make a lucid,
earnest, and feeling address, in which he explain-
ed very satisfactorily to his friends, after recount-
ing the misfortunes that had befallen him, the
causes that compelled him to abandon all further
attempts to continue longer so disastrous an ex-
periment.   He soon after played a short time at
the Chatham Theatre, and subsequently returned
to England.

For the next ten years, Mr. WALLACK played
star engagements in the United States and Great
Britain, in the meantime accepting the position of
leading actor and stage-manager, at the Princess's
Theatre in London, and there achieving one of his
greatest triumphs in the year 1843, as *Don Ceasar de Bazan.*

N. P. WILLIS, Esq., in writing from London, in
this year, says: "I have passed one evening of
great amusement at the Princess's Theatre, — WAL-
LACK playing in the two principal pieces. '*Don
Ceasar de Bazan*,' which you have had in America, was one of them, and it seems conceived and
written specially for this fine actor's peculiar pow-
ers.   The high-born Spanish gentleman, in pride
and rags, indomitably gay in his worst perils and
extremities, and preserving his elegance through
all his trials and tatters, could never be represented with more admirable truth and attractiveness.
The *abandon* with which WALLACK plays, seem-
ingly carried away by the gaiety of his part, yet
always true to nature and to the poet's meaning,
gives his performances, to me, a charm irresistible.
He was the attraction of the night, and the theatre
was crammed to suffocation."

Mr. WALLACK afterwards became stage-manager
of the Haymarket, where, in 1851, he introduced
to a London audience his nephew, Mr. J. W. WAL-
LACK, Jr., before referred to, and who resembles,
by the way, in a remarkable manner, his uncle, after whom he was named.   The likeness will appear still stronger to those who remember the latter twenty-five or thirty years since.

It was at this time that Mr. WALLACK was visited with a severe affliction, in the loss of his esti-
mable wife, and he himself was shortly afterwards
laid upon a couch of sickness, from which it was
feared he would never arise.

So serious, indeed, was his condition supposed,
that his son, Mr. LESTER WALLACK, then performing at Burton's Theatre in New York, received a
summons to London, urging his departure in the
mail steamer without delay.

But our actor's life was then spared, although
many months elapsed, before he could be pronounced convalescent.

Mr. WALLACK's last appearance in his native

land was at the Haymarket in the same year, per-
forming among other characters, *St. Pierre*, (in
Jas. Sheridan Knowle's play of the Wife,) to the
Mariana of Miss LAURA ADDISON, since deceased.

This brings us down to a period fraught with so
many pleasant memories connected with the theatres in which we of this latter day, have been so
wont to associate the name, genius, and liberality
of him who, as the "buried old man of seventy,"
our minds now and will ever, revert with mingled
regret and sorrow.

In the year 1851, he decided to permanently
make his home in this country, the scene of his
earlier joys and triumphs, and over nearly every
part of which he had travelled, steadily and deservedly gathering around him hosts of friends.

In 1852 he took possession of, and became the
manager of the theatre on Broadway, near Broome
Street, (formerly Brougham's Lyceum,) which he
conducted with uninterrupted success, and to the
advancement and improvement of which he unceas-
ingly devoted nine years.

The first performance under Mr. WALLACK's management, at that popular place of amusement, took place on the evening of September 8th, 1852, the whole interior of the house having undergone marked improvements, and presenting an elegant and inviting appearance.

The theatre was crowded to excess, and intense interest and enthusiasm was manifested in the success of our manager's undertaking.

At the conclusion of the excellent comedy, " *The Way to Get Married*," which was finely represented, having in the cast Messrs. LESTER WALLACK, BLAKE, WALCOT, Mrs. BUCKLAND, etc., etc., there was a unanimous call for Mr. WALLACK, and his appearance on the stage was a signal for the most vociferous and long-continued applause from the audience, many of his personal friends standing up, waving their hats and handkerchiefs, and shouting most energetically.   Having at length obtained silence, Mr. WALLACK addressed the audience as follows :

" LADIES AND GENTLEMEN : You are perhaps aware that I have suffered very much from ill health for the last two years, and this is the first time I have trod the boards of

a theatre for seventeen months. But, thank God, I am
well again. (*Cheers.*)

" I feel that respect for my audience should have induced
me to prepare a speech on this occasion; but I have not
studied one, and even if I had done so, it would have all
vanished from my brain when I came here among you,
and heard your applauses. Therefore, ladies and gentlemen, you must take it for granted that I mean sincerely
what I say, and you will forgive my want of eloquence,
since you have taken my feelings by storm. (*Loud Cheers.*)
It is now thirty years since I first appeared before a New
York audience. I was then in the young blood of life, and
I met with a reception like that which cheers me to-night.

" They hailed the young man with enthusiasm, and encouraged him as they do now the old man. He owes his
success to your kindness and forbearance, and, for thirty
years, in all the visits he has made, in all the branches of
his art, your enthusiasm and encouragement, your great
kindness and forbearance bore him up and furnished him
with greater power. He is happy to find the same feeling
towards him continued.

" Ladies and Gentlemen, I became a manager, as you
may remember. I am sure there are many here who remember the old National. You were pleased to approve of
my management then, and I trust experience as a manager,
in the little village of London, has since made me a little

more worthy of your patronage. (*Cheers.*) It is now thirteen years, since,— and I am certain you all regret it,— we lost that beautiful building by fire. It is, therefore thirteen years since I addressed you in the character of a manager, and it is five years since I acted before you. The National was a fine, gallant, first-rate old ship, full of all kinds of accommodations; but we have no doubt that this nice little frigate, with the noble and industrious hands to support her, will sail in the full favor of your approbation. (*Cheers.*)

"My object was to bring together those whom I knew to be established favorites with you. Most of them are here, and I will present to you soon, very soon, new candidates for your favor, and a few old ones, for I will act in a few days myself. (*Cheers.*) The style of our performances, ladies and gentlemen, will be high comedy, the highest and best class of farces, vaudevil, etc., dramas of stirring interest, such as the "Rent Day," "Don Ceasar de Bazan," etc. And we will give you novelties, new pieces. but no tragedy, much as I love it; for it was a tragedy I played in for the first fifteen visits out of nineteen, that I made to the United States.

"But my object is, to make you laugh, not to make you weep. It now remains to see how I will perform my promises to you. I know you will support me, and that I will be well supported by the company; I know that if I desire it, that I will get a portion of that favor which others

in the city so deservedly receive.   All I ask and sue for, is
a fair share, if I deserve it.   I go with the times ; but though
I have not the vanity to go before them, I am too quick to
be left behind.   (*Cheers.*)   If I gain your approbation, I
shall be content.   You will be satisfied, and I will see your
smiling faces till the last of the season."

Mr. WALLACK concluded this characteristic
speech amid tumultuous applause from all parts
of the house, and withdrew.   With the amusing
farce of the Boarding-School, in which the whole
company appeared, the entertainments of the evening terminated.

After inaugurating his own little play-house and
playing there a brief engagement, he, in November
following, appeared in Boston at the New National Theatre, (the old house, like its New York name-
sake, having been burned down a few years before.)

Mr. WALLACK had been engaged to perform at the
new theatre early in September, but the opening
night had been postponed, owing to a number of un-
foreseen circumstances, resulting most disastrously
for the worthy lessee, Mr. JOSEPH LEONARD.

Mr. WALLACK, with that courtesy which had ever distinguished him, wrote to the management, regretting that circumstances were as they were, and concluded by saying, "when you want me, let me know." At the appointed time therefore, November 22d, he was not found wanting.

Being always an especial favorite in Boston, he attracted on this occasion the most fashionable audiences and astonished his oldest friends, those who recollected him a quarter of a century ago, by his acting, which, in its artistic finish, seemed but little impaired by time.

His benefit was attended by the *élite* of the city, and being honored with a call before the curtain, he acquitted himself in a handsome manner, by speaking a good word for the management, a flattering notice of Mr. G. V. BROOKE, the well-known tragedian, whose engagement was to succeed his, and extended an invitation to all to visit him at WALLACK's Theatre in New York.

In the clever sketches of eminent performers, entitled "Actors as They Are," published in this city by Mr. ROORBACH, a few years ago, we find the following:

" Mr. WALLACK opened his theatre on Broadway under the most unfavorable circumstances. The company he had engaged was a large and expensive one,—the inauguration of his season had been unpromising,—thousands of dollars had been lost before the possibility of realizing one dollar had been presented. In this dilemma, Mr. WALLACK's company stood manfully by him. Theirs was a zeal removed entirely out of ordinary relations; and the result was, that the season terminated triumphantly."

As an evidence of the high esteem in which he was held, by those by whom he was surrounded in his professional duties, he was again, in the year 1855, tendered by the members of his own company, together with numerous other artists,—several of whom occupied the foremost position on the American stage,—a complimentary benefit.

This "Testimonial" took place on the afternoon and evening of May 29th, at the Academy of Music, on Fourteenth Street, and was one of the most successful demonstrations of the kind ever gotten up in this city.

Probably on no other occasion was so large an

audience ever convened within the walls of this magnificent building; the seats being all taken, and every available inch of standing-room closely contested.

The programme for the evening, included the names of Messrs. EDWIN FORREST and E. L. DAVENPORT, Miss VINING (now Mrs. E. L. DAVENPORT,) etc., etc., and consisted of Banim's well-known and popular play of "*Damon and Pythias*," and the fine English comedy of "*The Poor Gentleman*," since one of the standard attractions of "old WALLACK'S."

The acting of the first piece was undoubtedly the best ever seen in New York,—Mr. FORREST's performance of *Damon*, grand, dignified, noble, and impassioned,—while Mr. DAVENPORT's *Pythias* was a truly beautiful and judicious rendition of that favorite role.

Miss VINING played on this occasion, the difficult part of *Calanthe* with a great deal of power. Between the acts, and at the close of the play, Mr. FORREST, Mr. DAVENPORT, and Miss VINING, were severally called before the curtain to receive the acclamations of the delighted audience.

Mr. WALLACK then being vociferously called for, the veteran in a few moments appeared before the footlights, looking as hearty as ever, and acknowledged the plaudits of the audience with that exquisite grace which was one of the greatest charms of his acting.

When the excitement and enthusiastic demonstrations had subsided, he made a brief and pertinent speech, saying that he "had trusted to the occasion to inspire him, and that he was, therefore, altogether unprepared. Such triumphs as these," he continued, "were most grateful to the heart of the actor, who, by the peculiarity of his vocation, was prevented from having any test, other than the public voice, of the merit of his efforts.

"The painter or the sculptor could see and judge of the effect of his work after it had left his hands, but the successes of the actor were entirely ephemeral. After the triumph of a night, they passed away; therefore, the brilliant scene before him was the more gratifying to him, (Mr. WALLACK,) because it was a proof that his efforts had been appreciated."

In passing, he paid a graceful compliment to

Mr. FORREST, whom he called "*the* great tragedian of the American stage," and returned thanks to Mr. DAVENPORT, Miss VINING, and other artists, who had volunteered their services." He closed by saying that "this affair was a free-will offering to him, by his company and others of his profession, and he accepted it, *not* as some journals had hinted, as a *mendicant,* (it having been so represented in several of the newspapers of the day,) but as a *gentleman.* He had been over forty years connected with the stage, and thirty-seven years with American theatres, as an actor and manager. The public had had ample opportunities to judge of his merit in both positions, and he intended they should see more of him."

Mr. WALLACK then retired amid the most deafening applause.

The "Poor Gentleman," concluded the evening's performances, and was admirably played by the "Comedy company," the charming and accomplished *comedienne,* Mrs. HOEY, (so long the leading actress of WALLACK's theatre,) being substituted for Miss ROSA BENNETT who had been cast for *Emily Worthington,* but was prevented by illness from appearing.

The receipts on this occasion were variously es-
timated to have been from three to four thousand
dollars, and must have been highly gratifying to
Mr. WALLACK and his friends.

In the fall of this year, he made his re-appearance
for the first time, professionally, in twelve months,
on the occasion of the *complimentary benefit* extended to Mr. GEORGE H. BARRETT, (who does not
remember poor " *Gentleman George*," as " *Sir
Harcourt Courtly?*) on his final retirement from
the stage.

The voluntary aid proffered for this praiseworthy
object, numbered over one hundred of the principal performers in the country, the services of many of whom the committee were necessarily obliged
to dispense with, and those accepted were contrib-
uted chiefly by the Broadway and Wallack's theatres.

Mr. WALLACK, on this evening, (it being at the
Academy of Music, November 20th, 1855,) appeared in his beautiful impersonation of *Shylock*
in the "*Merchant of Venice*," supported by Madame PONISI, Mr. HENRY PLACIDE, etc.   The after-
piece was Sheridan's splendid comedy of the

"*School for Scandal*," Messrs. BLAKE, LESTER WALLACK, BROUGHAM, CHARLES FISHER, T. PLACIDE, Mrs. JULIA DEAN HAYNE, etc., performing, forming altogether a perfect and unequaled cast.

Previous to the comedy, Mr. BARRETT appeared before the curtain, having his children by the hand, and took leave of the public, in a short and feeling address.

As before stated, Mr. WALLACK enjoyed at his little theatre near Broome Street, an unvarying success for over nine years, during which period he was the acknowledged leader of dramatic art in America, and his theatre rose to a rank which no other had held in this community.

At this house closed his career as an actor, having performed there, within the above time, many of his principal characters, among which may be enumerated, *Shylock*, *Benedict*, (Much Ado About Nothing,) *Jaques*, (As You Like It,) *Martin Heywood*, (Rent Day,) *Erasmus Bookworm*, (The Scholar,) *Rover*, (Wild Oats,) *Sir Edward Mortimer*, (Iron Chest,) *Dick Dashall*, (My Aunt,) *Don Ceasar de Bazan*, etc., etc.

The first piece, "The Merchant of Venice," he produced on the night of the 9th of December, 1858, as a great Shakesperian revival, with new and superb scenery, costumes, properties, etc.

It had an unparalleled run; his rendition of the character of the "*merciless Shylock*," being universally commended, and eliciting the warm admiration of thousands who witnessed it, including representatives from all the departments of literature and the drama, and it was pronounced by all a chaste and beautiful performance.

The last representations in which he took part were at this theatre, where in 1859, he performed most of the above parts, besides sustaining for upwards of a hundred nights the leading character (*Colonel Delmar*,) in an exciting military drama, written by his son, Mr. LESTER WALLACK, entitled "*The Veteran*."

In 1861, he built his present Wallack's Theatre, on the corner of Broadway and Thirteenth Street, producing on the opening night a new play with an *apropos* title, ("The New President,") himself appearing at the close of the piece, in citizen's dress, to deliver a brief managerial address.

At the close of this season, (in 1862,) which was marked with the most unprecedented prosperity, he again appeared before the curtain, to address a few words to his numerous patrons and friends who assembled on this, as on all like occasions, in overflowing numbers.

This was his last appearance in any public capacity, and although it had been hoped that he might once more be enabled to delight and charm his many thousand admirers, by a repetition of his many beautiful impersonations, still, the increasing ailments attendant upon advanced age, and the too apparent symptoms of declining health and an impaired constitution, forbade all chances of the wishes of his friends being consummated.

Mr. WALLACK had been for several years in feeble health, suffering from a complication of diseases, among which gout and asthma were most prominent, and only a naturally strong constitution, and the most careful medical attendance, had enabled him so long to survive.

Several times within the past four years he had been pronounced at the point of death; but he rallied with unusual vigor after every attack, and regained strength from the sea-breezes of his Long Island villa.

It had been only within the past two or three months, however, that any serious apprehensions had been felt concerning the result of his illness, and until the beginning of the last week previous to his decease, he was in the habit of receiving visitors, and of personally directing the affairs of his theatre, so that the immediate occurrence of his death must have been almost entirely unexpected.

That mournful event, however, transpired but too soon and he died at his residence in Fourteenth Street, near Third Avenue, early on the morning of the 25th of December, 1864, "while the Christmas bells were chiming," and on the following Tuesday, his remains were consigned to the family vault in Greenwood Cemetery.

The funeral was conducted unostentatiously, and in a quiet manner, it being in accordance with the special request of the deceased.

Mr. WALLACK was about the medium height, gracefully proportioned, and possessing an air of dignity and intelligence. His dress was always scrupulously neat, and with the most fastidious taste, having somewhat of a Parisian appearance.

Of late years he walked with a cane, and a careful observer might have noticed that he pursued his steps toilsomely and with apparent difficulty.

He was, probably, up to the time of his retiring from the stage, the best of the old school of actors, and although critics might be disposed to question his genius in the highest walks of tragedy, still his eminence was a well-established fact, and his reputation was greatest in dramas of a romantic and picturesque order, in which his vigor, fire, and dashing energy, are said to have produced the most extraordinary effects.

His *Rolla* was great,—and universally pronounced an unrivalled performance of its kind,—his *Julian St. Pierre*, unapproachable;—his *Ruben Glenroy*, superb;—his *Benedict*, a masterpiece;—his *Shylock* and *Don Ceasar*, admirable.

In comedy and farce he also displayed great abilities, and the above characters will convey some idea of his peculiar and versatile talents.

As a manager, he has given us the best Comedy theatre in the country.

To say that Mr. WALLACK attained *perfection* in his theatrical management, would be crediting him with the accomplishment of an impossibility; but to say that he always *aimed* at perfection, and strove by every legitimate means within his grasp to secure it, and that the result of his endeavors was an elevation of theatrical intelligence and culture to a standard much higher than that achieved by any of his predecessors or cotemporaries, is the simple and universally recognized truth.

Mr. WALLACK's theatre has won the just reputation of being superior to any other in which the English language is spoken, and for this we have Mr. WALLACK alone to be grateful.

The material had all along been ready here, but the enterprise to rightly adjust and control it was wanting until he came.

He had learned, by long and varied experience, that the true way to command success in his profession is to thoroughly and honestly deserve it; and that although transient prosperity may follow startling departures from the golden theatrical rule, *enduring* fortune can only be gained by faithfully maintaining it.

The sense of his obligations and duties as a manager never forsook him, and he resolved that the last remainder of his failing strength should be devoted to the interest and protection of the art which he had loved and adorned, and which he had planted here in New York, upon the firmest basis ever known.

As a man, Mr. WALLACK had hosts of friends, and deserved them.

Cultivated and honorable, nothing offended him more than vulgarity, and nothing exasperated him more than over-reaching.

His dignity and simple courtesy were no less familiar to all who approached him, than the affability and generous feeling which inspired all his words and deeds.

Fond of a jovial, intellectual life, he delighted in merry, intelligent companions, and no one knew better than himself how to entertain others with wit, humor, and interesting conversation.

He was greatly attached to the profession of which he was such "a well-deserving pillar," and was full of reminiscences of the distinguished members of it, with whom he had come in contact in his long career. Possessed, too, of a kindly heart, his private charities were very large.

Among the members of his company he was held in the most enthusiastic affection, to all of whom his death will come as a personal affliction.

His fondness for children, too, was proverbial, being devotedly attached to his young grand-children; and God, in his infinite mercy and goodness, ordained that he should close his eyes in death with his favorites near him on Christmas day.

To those to whom he was thus endeared, and to his eldest son especially, — whose bereavement is nearer and more grievous, — the deepest sympathies of the community will be unfeignedly accorded. Thus has passed away from this earth, after "life's fitful fever," JAMES WILLIAM WALLACK, the most

accomplished of actors, and one of the most pol-
ished gentlemen on the stage.

> " Peace to his ashes! Distant realms combine,
> Lamented artist, thus to honor thine!
> Friends of the drama! Be it yours to mourn,
> And place fresh chaplets on the funeral urn;
> For your applause he ploughed the Atlantic wave,
> And found a welcome where he found a grave." (1)

In concluding this brief memoir, it may not be
improper to add that into the hands of his eldest
son, Mr. LESTER WALLACK, an American by birth,
and for so long the efficient stage-manager of his
theatre, has now passed the sole control of the
"comedy theatre," and that in those hands there
is every assurance of the same career of well-de-
served success being continued.

The following tribute of respect to the memory
of one whose loss as an *artist* it will not be possi-
ble to repair, any more than to fill the void as a
man, will not, I trust, be inappropriately append-
ed:

"At a meeting of managers of all the theatres
and places of amusement in New York, specially

convened at the Everett House, on Friday, December 30th, it was,—

"*Resolved,* That as a tribute of respect to the memory of JAMES W. WALLACK, *who did more than any one of his time to advance and elevate the drama, and who equally as a gentleman, a manager, and an artist, was for so many years the bright, particular ornament of our profession,* and also as a mark of sincere sympathy and regard for his son, Mr. JOHN L. WALLACK, the worthy inheritor of his cultivated taste and refined feeling, the managers of all the other theatres in New York will attend in a body at Wallack's Theatre, on Tuesday Evening, January 3d, being the occasion of the first appearance of Mr. JOHN L. WALLACK in a position in which we feel assured he will preserve the traditional honors that surround his name.(2)

"W. STUART, *Secretary.*"

NOTES.

(1) These lines, so appropriate at this time, are from a Monody written by a gentleman of Philadelphia in 1811 or 1812, on the occasion of the death of the celebrated tragedian, GEORGE FREDERIC COOKE, and which was delivered at the old Chestnut Street Theatre by Mr. DUFF.

(From the New York Times, Wednesday, January 4th, 1865.)

(2) WALLACK'S THEATRE. An enthusiastic welcome was extended last evening to Mr. J. LESTER WALLACK, who, after an absence from the stage, the cause of which every one laments, returned to it in the play of "Money," sustaining his well-known part of *Alfred Evelyn*. The event was celebrated by various marks of favor, which those who were present could appreciate more delicately than we can record. All true kindness, like sympathy, is unspoken. Suffice it that the house was crowded to its greatest capacity, and that Mr. J. LESTER WALLACK'S reception was so warm and significant that for a moment he was choked with an embarrassment, which, according to an old saying, brings the heart into the mouth. With a delicate geniality, which we cannot sufficiently admire, the proprietors and managers of all our principal places of amusement lent their presence to the occasion, extending, as it were, their hands—in a moment of mingled affection and consolation—to a comrade whom they have known long, and learnt to respect. The gentlemen referred to were Mr. STUART, of the Winter Garden; Mr. WHEATLEY, of Niblo's; Mr. GRAU, of the Italian Opera; Mr. FOX, of the Bowery Theatre; Mr. BARNUM, of the Museum; Mr. DAN. BRYANT, of Bryants' Minstrels; and Mr. WOOD, of Wood's Minstrels.

The performance was in every respect admirable, and the satisfaction expressed was complete. We shall, on another occasion, refer to the distribution. We desire now merely to join the common voice of satisfaction that receives Mr. J. LESTER WALLACK as the new manager of the theatre that his late father has made honorable to the art, and memorable in the annals of the American stage.